Praise for *Redshirts Sometimes Survive*

"I simply adore this book! It's a celebration both of *Star Trek* and of love in all its many forms. This bouquet of heartfelt flash fictions captures, better than any other work I've ever read, why *Star Trek* has endured as a cultural force for sixty years now: it's all about how, in this wide, wonderful universe of ours, there's a place for *everybody*. Written with empathy and wit, *Redshirts Sometimes Survive* moved me to both tears and laughter. Finnian Burnett is a national treasure."

–Robert J. Sawyer, Hugo Award-winning author of *The Downloaded*

"Hilarious, harrowing, and kind, *Redshirts Sometime Survive* delivers interconnected stories of apparently random and very diverse characters who all share one thing: a love of *Star Trek*. Pay attention, and you'll soon be taking in layered moments of both sorrow and joy, all layered with *Trek's* deep optimism. Never straying from hard realities, yet also never surrendering to despair, *Redshirts Sometimes Survive* is one gorgeous hopepunk book."

–Michelle Butler Hallett, disabled novelist and deep Trekkie, winner of the Thomas Raddall Atlantic Fiction Award, *Constant Nobody*

"*Star Trek* fans rejoice! In *Redshirts Sometimes Survive*, Finnian Burnett has written a love letter to all of us in the Bridge Crew who found family in other Trek fans. In writing that's both funny and heartbreaking, Burnett demonstrates how, in our shared love of Spock, Janeway, Picard and yes, even Kirk, we can find a community that we may not find elsewhere. But this novella-in-flash is much more than a celebration of a shared passion. In *Redshirts Sometimes Survive*, Burnett points out how *Star Trek* calls us to action, to speak out, to protest, to stand up to bullies as Captain Janeway would. Because here, in the *Star Trek* universe, we can imagine a world where we're accepted as we really are. If we can imagine that, Burnett suggests, then we can also make it so."

—Gail Anderson-Dargatz, bestselling author of *The Almost Widow*

"Burnett expertly draws us away from the expectation of inevitable Redshirt dispensability and instead builds a diversity of narratives around the treks of the marginalized. These episodes-in-flash feature queer found family and crushes, a child put through the system, a nonspeaking disabled elder who recalls the TOS days, the desire for fat bodies sharing adventures, and even Star-crossed fandoms. A must-have collection for geeks of all generations."

—Cait Gordon, award-winning author of *Season One: Iris and the Crew Tear Through Space!*

"*Redshirts Sometimes Survive* is truly Trek: a smorgasbord of humanity, full of found family and queer self-love, designed to help us envision all of ourselves."

—Murgatroyd Monaghan, winner of the Pacific Spirit Poetry Prize, *white spaces where we learn to breathe*

"Much like the Federation, this book shows us that our differences can only make us stronger if we're brave enough to reach for the stars."

—Peter J. Foote, author of *Eclipsing the Aurora*

"Beautifully queer, heart-warming and poignant. One moment these stories leave you gasping for breath and then the next floating on a cloud."

—Robin van Eck, author of *Rough*

Redshirts Sometimes Survive

by Finnian Burnett

Off Topic Publishing

First print edition: April 2026 by Off Topic Publishing

Paperback ISBN: 978-1-0698344-0-9
eBook ISBN: 978-1-0698344-1-6

Edited by Marion Lougheed
Cover Design: Jelena Mirkovic Jankovic | IG: @boja99designs

Off Topic Publishing: www.offtopicpublishing.com

Previous Publication Credits:

"When Captain Picard Was My Dad" by Pulp Literature. 2023.
"Satan Gets in Through the Cracks" by Blank Spaces Magazine. 2023.
"Ethan Peck's Muscles" (as "Ethan's Pecs") by Pulp Literature. 2023.
"Two Men Kissing" by the London Independent Story Prize. 2023.
"Life Capacity" by Blank Spaces Magazine. 2023.
"Red Shirts Sometimes Survive" by Free Flash Fiction. 2022.
"A Moon More Beautiful" by Storybilder. 2021.

For my wife, August van Stralen, who shares both my love of writing and my love of Star Trek, to the small group of weirdos who make up my found family, and to everyone who hasn't yet found theirs.

Contents

Ethan Peck's Muscles

Ethan Peck flexes his muscles on the screen and Candice sighs. *He's so dreamy, so tall, so gorgeous*, she says next to me. It's not the actor she loves, it's Spock, the character he plays—that's what I tell myself when Candice says, "Isn't he perfect?" And he is, he's perfect, so perfectly male and Candice's hands rub circles on the thighs of her jeans as Ethan speaks his deep-voiced logic, tightly controlled emotion simmering under the surface and Candice leans toward the TV, eyes wide, and Ethan's such a man, such a deep-voiced man and I slide deeper into my oversized button-front shirt trying to hide the side-boob flab that has escaped my binder.

She falls in love with him over and over when he comes on the screen and *I'm right here*, I want to say, but instead, I watch the show and listen to Candice's sighs and when it's over, she rubs her fingers over my sparse new beard and says, "I love you, Devin."

And she does. Even through my tortured doubts, I know she truly does.

Teddy and His Lunch Ladies

Teddy was quiet, well-behaved. He'd come to the lunch counter in an oversized Star Trek shirt that might have belonged to an older brother or one that, maybe, he found in a donation box at church. And he'd ask for a biscuit, maybe, or a slice of bread. But we gave him free lunches, without telling anyone, and we asked about his day and when Marge noticed the holes in his shoes, we went to the thrift store and found the best of the used shoes we could find.

You can't be expected to notice everything, but we noticed the way the kid stood with his hands in his pockets, the circles under his eyes that got deeper and darker, the yellow and purple bruises that came and faded and came and faded. The way the Star Trek shirt got older and dirtier and how, when Teddy sat at a table by himself, he'd curl into it and almost disappear as he ate his free lunch.

One day, Ayala found a beat-up Spock figure in the street on her way to work and she brought it to school, and we furtively washed it in the kitchen between lunch shifts. When Teddy came to the cafeteria, we tucked little Spock onto his tray and he looked up at us, tears in his eyes and we knew he meant it when he said, "Thank you."

It might have been Mina who said, "I wish we could adopt him," and we shushed her and clucked our tongues while we watched him eating his lunch with one hand, holding his Spock figure in the other, and staring at it with wonder, as we stared with wonder at him.

We served him shepherd's pie and offered extra napkins because we knew how messy he was and, in a way, we thought of him as our own son, this child of the lunch ladies, and we talked offhand about buying him a new Star Trek shirt someday, and we told ourselves we were doing our best for him and it wasn't until he stopped coming to school that we realized we hadn't done nearly enough.

Redshirts Sometimes Survive

Danny wears command red with three pips, though inevitably someone will say, "Better be careful beaming down to the planet in that red shirt, little lady—har har." Like we haven't heard that dozens of times, like the redshirt thing wasn't old before *The Next Generation* even premiered, like Danny hasn't been misgendered a thousand times in a thousand different places. Danny, with his new belly meat squashed out from the ill-fitting binder we bought second-hand on Marketplace, wants to look like season-two Commander Riker even though Danny's T-induced beard is sparse and splotchy and, if I'm being honest, he looks more like Wesley Crusher than Commander Riker.

At the convention, we push into the line of people waiting for autographs, ignoring the redshirt jokes, and wait under the sign that says *No Pictures*.

"What if he hates me," Danny says.

"He won't."

"What if he does?"

The crush of bodies is suffocating and when the crowd around us swells tighter, I fight the urge to drop Danny's hand and run for the door. But Danny needs me, and I practice deep breathing as we inch and inch and inch forward and when we're finally at the table, Danny puts a picture on the table in front of Jonathan Frakes and his voice cracks when he says, "I know we're not allowed pictures." His voice is shaking, and I want to drag him out of there, make him safe, but Danny takes a deep breath. "But you took this picture with me when I was someone else."

Danny squeezes my hand so tightly; I'm losing blood in my fingers, and his lower lip trembles the way it does when he's either close to a panic attack or so near to tears that the slightest quiver could set off a deluge.

Jonathan looks at the picture. It says, "To S_____ with love." He looks back up, smiles, and says, "I guess we should take a new one." And when he says to Danny, at the end, that "It's okay to cry," Danny does just that—a deluge, all over his red shirt.

Two Men Kissing

This is a family company. These words echo in my head while I watch *Discovery* with my family and when Stamets and Dr. Hugh kiss, I see only Jamie Buckman's gang screaming out the car windows and my first girlfriend asking what she'd done wrong and my father's belt on the back of my legs. My mother throwing my backpack out the front door, *Come back when you're normal,* and the stone-hard backs of men on the other side of bar nights and *This is a family company* tossed across my boss's desk with my last paycheque and my husband's hurt face when I yanked my hand from his as my parents finally opened their door—the well-meaning smiles from other parents at our son's daycare, *Aren't they a cute couple,* someone whispers, and the teacher asking, *Which one of you is the father?* And my mother holding her first grandson, *He's going to turn out just like you.* The kids at softball laughing because our child has two goddamn dads and how we're all sitting on the couch watching two men kiss on Star Trek and my son turns around smiling and says, *Just like my dads.* My husband's hand is warm in mine as he leans in and in this moment, for this moment, we're only ourselves, two men kissing.

Wesley Crusher Faces His Fear

Turn off the fucking TV, my mom yells from her bedroom, even though it's Star Trek, even though it's a Wesley episode and I haven't seen this one yet.

But Mom's been working night shifts, and she doesn't like loud noises when she's trying to sleep so my sisters and I take our bowls of cereal and sneak down to the basement to watch the rest of the show on the little black and white television down there.

The basement is creepy. It smells like mould, and you get fleas all over your ankles when you walk down there because of the stray dog we brought home who needs to go to the vet but we asked our mom to take us and Susie got spanked. So we've stopped asking.

The dog curls up on a dirty blanket next to the scratchy yellow and brown couch we pulled from the neighbour's garbage and dragged down here while Mom was at work one night. The TV screen flickers and the static hums louder than the show, and we're so cold, we're shivering, but I don't care because Wesley's on screen and he's taking the Starfleet Academy exam.

In the simulation, which Wesley doesn't know isn't real, the room is depressurizing, and a man is pinned under debris. Another is panicking. Wesley has to decide who to save.

And he hesitates because he doesn't know what to do, and I'm holding my breath because I know how it feels to realize that no matter what choice you make, it's going to hurt.

Wesley saves one man and lets the other one die.

As he stands, stunned, in the corridor, an admiral comes to tell him it was all a fake. A chance to see how he'd react in a situation much the same as the one that killed his father, when Captain Picard had to choose to save one and leave the other. The other was Wesley's father.

Wesley realizes he had to face his fear, his greatest fear, the fear of making the wrong choice and leaving someone to die. And the camera closes in on his face and my sisters and I sit, stunned, forgetting for a moment we're sitting in a cold basement with flea-bitten legs, and bowls of cereal in our laps.

Because I know exactly how he feels.

He's afraid of letting someone down.

And I'm afraid of letting *everyone* down.

Wesley lost his dad on a mission. And I've lost my mom to my fear of her—fear of her anger, her hitting, her drunkenness, her everything.

Wesley's dad is never coming back because he's dead. And for a moment, I wish my mom was dead, too.

I slap my hand over my mouth like the thought might come out, like my sisters might gasp in horror, like God himself might strike me down with lightning.

But none of that happens. I don't speak, none of my sisters react, and Wesley goes on to learn he didn't make it into the academy this time. Not because of something he did wrong, but simply because someone else performed a little bit better.

As the episode ends, my sisters and I sit, transfixed, scratching flea bites on our legs and wishing we could somehow slink into the TV, run away with Wesley and go away with him where no kids—at least, no kids like us—have gone before.

Teddy Checks In

We watch him shift from foot to foot at the entry desk, beat-up backpack hanging off oneshoulder. He's wearing a threadbare Star Trek T-shirt and he's clutching a Spock action figure so hard his knuckles are white. Someone, maybe Mildred, says, "He's too soft for this place," and we don't answer because we know it can strip a kid of softness, being here.

The intake clerk says the kid's name, Teddy, and we want to weep. Teddy, who needs a friend and a hug and maybe a new Star Trek T-shirt, one that doesn't look as if the dirt and tears of a thousand years has been ground into it, won't get any of that here.

Don't touch the kids, don't get involved, for god's sake, don't feel sorry for anyone, because if you let your heart break once, it will never stop breaking.

We look away from the kid, from this Teddy, as he's led to his room and someone, maybe Mildred again, says, "I saw a Star Trek shirt on clearance at Kid's Depot the other day." But no, we tell her. Not for this one. Not for any of them.

Satan Gets in Through the Cracks

Mama works nights and sends us to Mrs. Bloom's for dinner and sleep. On the hottest nights, Mrs. Bloom lets us drag sleeping bags to the screened-in porch where we fall asleep listening to the peepers, the owls, and a scratchy growl Benny thinks is a monster. Mrs. Bloom's toothless boyfriend, Tank, says it's just a mama badger clucking at her babies.

Benny stops under the badger crossing sign and asks if I think we'll see a badger tonight.

"No, Benny." I take her hand to keep her moving. We never see badgers. We never see anything good—just deer most of the time, and sometimes yellow-bellied marmots if we go outside early enough.

Benny wrenches from my grip and drops to her knees behind the bumper of Gordon McNabb's van, the big tan one with a spray-painted naked lady on the side, one Mama says we should never get in because old Gordon's full of sin and so is his van.

"Come on from there," I hiss. But she's half under the bumper and she screeches like a baby monkey when I grab her leg.

"Stop, Lainey!" she yells, kicking back. I squat on the driveway behind her, looking around for either Gordon or Mama, not sure which one would be worse.

"Benny," I whisper through gritted teeth, "If you don't come out from there—right now—I swear to God I'm telling Mama."

"Don't swear to God," she says. "It's a sin." She scrambles out and jumps to her feet. Her knees are pitted with gravel and dirt. I send up a quick prayer of thanks that we're on our way to Mrs. Bloom's, and not home, because Mrs. Bloom will wash Benny's knees with a warm cloth and maybe give her a popsicle. She'll let Benny put on pants, pants that Mrs. Bloom's only son used to wear when he was little, so she doesn't get dirty running around outside.

"I found a Data," Benny squeals, holding up a hard plastic figurine, half-covered in mud. It is Data, one of her favourite Star Trek characters—I guess. It's hard to tell through the mud, but the yellow and black Star Trek uniform looks about right and if anyone would know, it would be Benny.

"Can I keep it?" She stares at me, eyes solemn. "Please, Lainey."

It's the devil, I can hear my mom saying. Everything is from hell if you listen to our mom. Starships, phasers, television, Tommy Decker from down the street, Gordon's van, Gordon, frozen food, braces, medicine, wearing pants. *Satan gets in through the cracks left when we sin,* Mama says.

I take the Data figure and rub some of the dirt off with my hand. "You can keep it," I say, handing it back to her. "But you can't tell Mama."

She takes it and holds it to her cheek. "I can't wait to show Tank."

Mama doesn't know we watch Star Trek at Mrs. Bloom's house after playtime, when we come in from running in the yard. Before we come in to watch Star Trek, we look for animals in Mrs. Bloom's big backyard that butts up against Crown land and has a river running through it.

Tank swears there's foxes and badgers and flying squirrels and coyotes there, right in their own backyard. Some nights, he comes out with us and builds a fire in the big pit, and as the sun goes down, he tells us all about all the animals he's seen on his camping trips—like bears and moose, and even a wolverine once.

As we search for animals, Mrs. Bloom sits on her porch and smokes, smiling over us, only calling us in when it's full dark and we're covered with mosquito bites. She makes us frozen dinners—Tank's favourite—even though Mama sends us with peanut butter sandwiches because she's not paying extra for Mrs. Bloom's food. We watch Star Trek with Tank who loves Mrs. Bloom even though she and Mr. Bloom, who lives in Alberta, are still married. We love Tank, even with his missing teeth that he swears he lost fighting a wolverine. He works at the plant and has a tattoo of a motorcycle on his bicep that moves when he flexes, like when he shares his cherry cobbler with me.

Mama says tattoos are from the devil. She also says Satan loves complainers when we whine about being hungry, when we tell her she's hurting us, when we cry about wearing hand-me-downs at school. Mama says Jesus wore hand-me-downs and aren't we a couple of ingrates. Her fingers leave uneven trails of bruises on our arms. Mama's anger flares when we talk about Mrs. Bloom, so we don't talk about her, and instead, we wait for her to sleep so we can go to our room and whisper about the show we watched at Mrs. Bloom's.

Benny skips along next to me, swinging one arm, the other holding Data to her face like a candle. At times, she holds him away and looks at him, beaming, and I imagine her all lit up and radiant-like. Not all candles are bad. I wonder if she's old enough to remember the time when Tank bought her a Captain Picard figure and how Mama screamed when she found it, cursing that Benny must have done something unspeakably bad for Tank to get that toy and how I said the only person who ever tried to touch us that way was her preacher after he asked me to light the candles at church. Mama beat me so hard I couldn't go to school for a week.

"Just please don't let Mama find it," I tell Benny again and she looks up at me, sad and silent. She gives a nod and I think, *She remembers. How could she forget?*

On Sundays, Mama doesn't go to work. "It's a day of rest," she says, but it's not. We go to church, and they give us a box of food in exchange for us making the place look nice. When we get home, we pray, and Mama reads the Bible and reminds us that sin is everywhere, even in little children. She inspects our fingers and stares into our eyes. Sometimes, she sees something she doesn't like so she gets out the belt. *You have to squash the sin before it starts*, she says. We eat rice and beans and open dented cans that other people have donated. Sometimes we eat spaghetti with lima beans. Sometimes, canned potatoes and tomato soup.

Benny runs up the stairs of Mrs. Bloom's house and pounds on the door with one hand, the other still clutching her treasured Data figurine. As soon as Mrs. Bloom lets us in, she runs to Tank and shows him the toy.

"That's a good one," he says, with his endearing missing-tooth grin. "Data's my favourite."

"Mine too!"

Tank teaches me to play cards while Mrs. Bloom cleans Benny's knees and washes her new toy. She lets us go outside with Tank to look for animals and, in the dusk, right before Mrs. Bloom stubs out her cigarette, Benny spots three moose on the other side of the river. Mrs. Bloom slips quietly from the porch and Tank puts his arm around her. We pull closer to them, Benny and I, holding hands, and we watch mama moose and her babies. For a moment, I dream about running away to live here with Mrs. Bloom and Tank and the moose, but Mama would know where we were, here where Satan comes in through the cracks. When the moose family leaves, Tank puts his hand on Benny's shoulder and tells her that in Star Trek, no one goes hungry and no one ever hurts little kids. Never.

And never is a long time. But right now we have Mrs. Bloom. And Tank. And Data.

When Captain Picard Was My Dad

When I didn't make the kickball team, Captain Picard didn't say, "I'd hoped at least one of my kids wasn't a loser." He didn't say that at all. He didn't tell me I'd make the team next year if I'd only lose some goddamned weight because an oinker like me couldn't keep up with the other third graders. Captain Picard told me you can do your best and still lose and he believed I did my best. He said I should be proud of myself, even if no one else was proud of me.

When Captain Picard was my dad, I didn't get beaten with a yardstick after I was suspended in the fourth grade. I didn't get thrown into my bedroom without dinner and I didn't lie awake all night to the throbbing of my burgeoning bruises. After all, when Will Riker violated the Treaty of Algernon, Captain Picard told him that the important thing was not what he'd done in the past, but what he was going to do going forward. Will almost started a war with the Romulans and all I did was write *Fuck school* on the wall of the second-floor bathroom, the one beside the chemistry lab, but Captain Picard forgave us either way.

Captain Picard never said fat girls should have nicer personalities and fat girls don't have to be strong because they can sit on their enemies and he never, ever said, "Whoa, my god, it's coming toward me!" Captain Picard never smashed my head into the garage door or pulled out a handful of my hair or threw the remote at me so hard it left a gash and then a scar on my eyebrow. And when Captain

Picard was my dad, I didn't wear long sleeves and jeans in the summer.

When Captain Picard was my dad, I didn't have to sit bedside of someone I hated, didn't hear the skeleton breath of someone who was dying but not fast enough, didn't bite my tongue as my deadname rattled again and again from bone-dry lips that could only spew hate and never love. I didn't clutch my arms against my sides to keep anxiety from eating me alive. I didn't pretend the scars disappeared with the bruises. I didn't have to do it, none of it, not when Captain Picard was my dad.

What Would Janeway Do?

She'd order coffee. She'd get coffee from the replicator, and when she couldn't get it from the replicator, she'd drink some of Neelix's homebrewed sludge. She'd put on a tank top, arm herself, and hit them with everything she had.

What would I do? What I always do. What I've always done. Nothing.

Nothing Nelly, my mom always calls me.

Nothing Nelly never goes anywhere except once I went to a Trek convention. Nothing Nelly even paid to get into the line to get *her* autograph, to tell *her* that I wanted to be her, to ask *her* how she always knew the right thing to say, how *she* got people to pay attention even though she was smaller than them. She was pretty. As I stood in the line, some people around me argued over whether Kirk was a better leader than Picard and someone else said Sisko and then someone said, "Janeway is a war criminal," and I couldn't open my mouth. They'd stood right there next to me, right there in her line and talked about all of Janeway's mistakes and I wanted to shut them up but as usual, Nothing Nelly couldn't say a word.

But then, when it was my turn, she smiled at me. She said, "Thank you for coming. It means a lot."

But it could have meant more. I hadn't stood up for her. Not in person right there in front of her. Not even in forums. *Janeway was the worst captain*, someone writes, and I don't respond.

I never respond. I can't make my fingers type the words, can't find a way to stand up for someone I care about, someone who embodies everything I wish

I was. I'm like one of those background characters who never gets a line, but you know when they show up in a shuttle with one of the main characters, they're about to die.

Nothing Nelly never says a word.

And then *they* came into power.

The ones making legislation proving people I love and care about don't have rights. The ones putting innocent people into prisons and camps. The ones harming everyone who disagrees with them. And I disagree with them.

Laws are changing so fast I can't keep up. On the forums, my friends talk about political action, non-violent protests, writing to lawmakers, writing op-eds. I don't know how to write an op-ed. I don't know how to do anything.

What would Janeway do?

Janeway would speak up. Janeway wouldn't side with Nazis and fascists. But I'm not the kind of person who speaks up. I'm not a leader. I'm not important. To anyone. Not even to myself.

But what would Janeway do?

She'd drink coffee. She'd drink coffee and talk to her team, and she'd find a way to sort things out because no matter what anyone else thinks of Janeway, she cares about what's right and she believes in peaceful solutions. Janeway always looks for a diplomatic solution—*until there isn't one.* Janeway, who fought and beat the Borg Queen; Janeway, who put Tuvix in the transporter to save the lives of two people she loves even when her own doctor refused to participate; Janeway, who once told an entire species *I don't like bullies, I don't like threats, and I don't like you.*

What would Janeway do?

***

I don't bring a sign.

The protesters stand on the steps of city hall, but I hang back, hands in my pockets. Others chant, yell, jump onto each other's shoulders to see over the crowd.

An older woman in a tank top, clearly lacking a bra, turns and smiles at me. Her sign says *Make America Think Again*. She's glorious, like an older Janeway, and if she'd been toting a type-3 compression rifle instead of a sign, I'd expect her to drop to the ground, roll and fire at the enemy, vanquishing them. She'd then come home to tell the tale of her victory and make some hot coffee.

Instead, she pushes through the crowd, and I lose sight of her. I grab a milk crate and jump on it, looking through the sea of signs and I spot her, long grey hair in several braids down her back, sign held high over her head. She's yelling and my heart nearly explodes. With fear, yes, but something else. Something . . . deeper. And then she's gone—shoved and knocked down. A guttural yell surges from the crowd and the cops move in. The officer kicks at someone and I hear a high-pitched scream. It's her. I can't know this from here, but I do anyway.

They just kicked my Captain Janeway. MY Captain. And I am burning with Janeway-level rage, like the fury she unleashed on the Borg, like the way she took down the Kazon, like the way she told

Callah she didn't like bullies, and I, for once in my life, I'm not that quiet one standing in line with an Admit One ticket tucked up my sleeve so I don't lose it. I'm not putting up with people fucking about with MY Captain. I'm running through the crowd, pushing through the press of bodies, not away from the conflict but toward it, toward danger, toward the screaming cries of the *Make America Think Again* woman and suddenly I'm through the crowd—now standing in front of the cops as everyone pushes past me, around me. I'm almost knocked down, but I plant my feet and I stare into the faceless mask of the alien in front of me. "I don't like bullies!" I'm screaming, and a cop pauses in front of me. I'm going to get hit, or knocked down, or thrown down and placed in handcuffs or plastic ties, and I don't care because I know what Janeway would do and it's exactly this.

The woman with the grey braids is on the ground in front of me. She has her hands up to shield her face and I reach down to grab them, to help her up. She hands me her sign first and I take it with one hand while I hold out the other. Our hands connect. A jolt runs through me, like dammit, this is my time, like I know, for the first time maybe in my entire life, I'm doing exactly what I should be.

"What would Janeway do!" I yell, but I know the answer. She'd do this.

I pull the woman up to stand next to me and, together, we wrap our hands around the base of the sign. The cop doesn't shrink back, but he doesn't knock me down. The crowd thrums around me, a living thing with voices and hands and tears and fury and the *Make America Think Again* woman presses against me and her braids brush against my hand and I clench my thigh muscles, plant my feet, and open my mouth.

"I don't like bullies!" I yell again.

The woman smiles.

"What's your name?" she cries out.

"Nelly. My name is Nelly."

What would Nelly do, I think for a moment, but now I know the answer. Nothing Nelly no more.

"My name's Jane!"

Of course it is. I raise the sign for all to see.

Teddy Finds a Home

We watch him explore his room—his own room. He stands in the doorway first, eyes tracking over the walls, the desk, the row of shelves we've left mostly empty so he can fill them himself. He does see the Star Trek action figures we've tucked away on the second bottom shelf, the ones we bought before we brought him home. A corner of his mouth twitches, but he doesn't say anything. His eyes move to the dresser, the bed, the comfy chair we've set up in the corner, the one with the ottoman, and a side table because we thought he might want to sit and read or talk on the phone or just exist sometimes in private.

"Teddy," I say, breaking the silence, and he turns to look at us. He's near tears and we can't decide whether we should leave him alone or continue to hover. We are new to parenting, let alone helicopter parenting. Finally, we tell him to come find us if he needs help unpacking or when he's ready to eat lunch.

We sit at the kitchen table, holding hands, and Maris reminisces about the first time we met him, how the three of us bonded over our favourite Star Trek characters. Him, Spock. Me, Jean Luc Picard, Maris, Lwaxana Troi. How Maris had cried on the way home, how it wasn't fair for such a kind boy to have had such a hard life, how she wanted to foster him, perhaps adopt him and how I'd said no because I wanted a baby or a toddler, someone we could grow to love and what could a couple of middle-aged lesbians have in common with a pre-teenage boy from a juvenile home.

We'd gone back to visit him again and again in that Borg ship of social services—watching his personality slowly being assimilated into hopelessness and despair and Maris, on the day social services called and said, "We have a baby you might want to meet," put her foot down. She said, "I can't live without him."

And I said, "Give this baby a chance," and we went to meet her, and the social worker said there were already ten couples on the list to adopt but we were number one—and Maris whispered, "How many people are on Teddy's list?"

I didn't answer because I knew without asking. And I kissed the baby, the one who would go on to have a wonderful life with someone who wasn't me, and I turned to Maris. "If you can't live without him," I said before kissing her. "Then make it so."

Romulans Stole Our Dad

He hits me with his phaser. *Pew. Pew.* He's yelling as he dives behind a tree. *Pew pew.* I'm supposed to fall dead now, or stunned, I guess. But I'm playing a different game. He's Kirk on an away mission and I'm Geordi LaForge, taking a walk on the holodeck on the first day of spring, waiting for my friends to join me, but enjoying the alone time while I'm waiting.

Pew! He screams again and, "Callie, come on!"

"I told you," I yell back. "We're *Next Generation* today."

He slumps, defeated. I give in to his requests every few days, turning our games into a free-for-all shootout. I play whatever villain he's chosen for the day, and it always ends with him shooting me with the stick he's designated his phaser while I scream and beg for mercy.

I lean back against the tree, letting its rough bark brush against my elbows. Pete finally gives up and crawls over to sit next to me. "I just want to play Star Trek," he says.

I feel guilty, sorry for my little brother who hasn't yet figured out why our father doesn't live here anymore, why our mom leaves every night, why I get tired of trying to figure out meals, get him dressed, act as a substitute for parents who never had time for him anyway. I had a decade with them before Pete came along. Were they ever happy? I remember our dad taking me to a Star Trek convention, both of us in matching uniforms, all the people telling me how cute I was.

Pete will never get to experience that.

I put my arm around him. "We are playing Star Trek," I tell him, measuring my words carefully. "We're on the holodeck, getting ready for Captain Picard's birthday."

"Captain Picard is gone," he says, tears nearer the surface now.

He is gone, you just need to accept it, I want to tell him. But I don't. Instead, I grab his hand, hard and lean in to whisper urgently. "He was taken by the Romulans."

Pete flips around to stare, the threat of tears gone in the excitement of the idea. "Romulans stole him?"

"It's the god honest truth." I hold up my fingers in a Vulcan salute. "I swear on Spock."

Pete doesn't care when I mix my Star Treks. It doesn't matter. All that matters is Captain Picard is missing. "Callie," he says. "We've got to go find him."

I push myself off the ground and reach for his hand. "Let's do that, Pete. Let's just do that."

Must Love Star Trek

Must love Star Trek, their Tinder profile said, and also *they/them* and *progressive* and *sex positive* and into Victorian women poets plus they love cats and Terry Pratchett, and their profile picture on Insta, because I stalked them by their username, is of Captain Janeway so of course I swiped right. We're sitting in my favourite restaurant and we both ordered mocha lattes with oat milk and we've laughed out loud and our fingers touched and I just about died when we found out we both thought the movie version of *Lord of the Rings* was better than the books, but *The Chronicles of Narnia* movies didn't come close to the originals and I want to kiss them but before I can muster up the nerve, they ask me, *Who's your favourite Captain?* and I say *Captain Pike* before I can think and they pull their hand away. *What about Janeway?* And I say, *I have a thing for hot but affable father figures*, and they look at me for a long moment in that *I-like-you-and-you-are-adorable-but-that-just-won't-do* sort of way before asking for the cheque.

Make It Soap

The conference was supposed to be about Star Wars. Adam had slammed the flyer down onto Cade's desk in fourth-period English. Mark Hamill smiling in the middle. *Meet Luke Skywalker*, the flyer said, and so when Adam said, *Come to the con with me*, had even offered to drive and pay for parking, Cade had to, of course, say yes, not just because of Mark Hamill or the free ride with free parking, but because of Adam. There wasn't much Cade wouldn't do for Adam, except love Star Trek, apparently, because try as they might, they just couldn't fall in love with it the way Adam had.

But they said yes because of Adam, because of Mark Hamill, because of the excitement of moving through a crowd of nerds of every fandom. People who understood.

And here they are, weaving through a crowd of excited fans like a professional stormtrooper, fast, disorganized, and able to miss all of the targets in front of them. Adam turns back to smile and Cade's heart pounds. From the excitement, they tell themself, but Adam's glowing face, the shine in his eyes, strengthen the beat. Adam is in a group of people wearing Star Trek uniforms and he's trying to make friends, Cade can tell, but Adam can be awkward. Cade presses their shoulder against Adam's arm and smiles at the group.

They recognize pointed ears, if nothing else. This will be easy. "Ah, you're Spock," Cade says, throwing out one of the maybe three Star Trek names they know.

"I'm clearly Next-Gen era Sarek," the person responds.

Cade inwardly groans, but Adam grins. "My bestie," he says. "Not much of a fan."

Cade notes the pasted-on smiles of the group, how they turn from Cade and Adam. "What's your favourite ship?" Cade asks frantically before the group can disband. And suddenly, they're all chattering and Adam's part of the crowd of people shouting, "Defiant!" "Bird of Prey!" "D!"

And Adam's arm is warm against Cade's and they don't have anything to add to the conversation, but Adam is happy. Cade can feel Adam's joy thrumming through their joined bodies.

Someone asks, "What's your thing, then?"

Cade says, "Star Wars" and the crowd collectively groans. But Cade says, "We're not that different. We have the Death Star. You have the Death Cube."

First, there is silence.

Then a guy in a red Starfleet uniform gasps so loudly he starts coughing.

Another pointy-eared person staggers backward, clutching their chest like they've been shot.

"Excuse me?" a woman in a leather costume shrieks, knocking over her own drink.

One guy drops to his knees like he's been wounded–the dagger thrust in, waiting now for it to be withdrawn.

"DON'T YOU MEAN THE BORG CUBE?" the person in the Sarek costume says, their voice shaking with emotion.

Cade shrugs. "What's the difference?"

A man with giant forehead ridges howls in despair.

"Oh, now you've done it," Sarek moans. "You've gone and upset the Klingon."

"Oh my god, Cade," Adam says, burying his face in his hands. "Why hast thou forsaken me?"

Cade tries to smile. "Beam me out, Scotty."

Adam groans and the crowd around them disperses, maybe because of Cade, or maybe because of the announcement that drones on about them having to stand in line for autographs. Cade wants to go find Mark Hamill, but more than that, they want Adam to be happy.

"I'm sorry. I'm here and I'm trying," Cade says. They are trying, trying as hard as they can. Not because they love Trek but because they love Adam, because Adam deserves people who care about his passions. "I get why this is a big deal," Cade adds, "but I can't make myself someone I'm not."

"I know," Adam says. "And I do appreciate the effort."

"If you want," Cade says, "I can try again. I can watch a different Trek, try to get more into things like teleporters and warp kale."

"Coils."

"Kale. Coils. Whatever." As soon as this con is over, Cade will watch every Star Trek there is, force themself through every episode, learn all the lingo. Whatever they have to do to get closer to Adam. "Come on," Cade says. "Let's go stand in line to get that robot's autograph."

"That's Data. And he's an android." Adam takes Cade's hand. "But you came here to see Mark Hamill. So, let's do that first."

Cade luxuriates in the feel of Adam's hand, in the way Adam's fingers twine through theirs.

"We don't have to love the same things," Adam says. "In a way, we're like Kirk and Spock." At Cade's blank look, he goes on. "They were the best of friends, but they were wildly different. They complemented each other. They made each other better." He pauses, stopping to smile at Cade. "Just like us."

The wounded Klingon wanders by, still shaking his head. "Death Cube," he mutters as he stomps past them.

Adam watches the Klingon for a moment, then turns back. He leans forward and draws Cade toward him, grabbing them softly by the shoulders. "They made each other better," he says, again before kissing Cade softly on the mouth. "Just like us."

Cade can't breathe. Flummoxed, they blink up at Adam. "Oh wow. What would Captain Peckard say?"

Adam grins. "Captain Picard would probably say 'Make it soap.'"

"Then make mine a double," Cade says.

And Adam kisses them again.

One Last Frontier

"Take your meds, honey," the nurse says, handing you the paper dispensing cup while holding a cup of water for you to sip. You've lost your ability to hold it, your trembling fingers having lost their grip. Not the first thing you've lost. Not even the most recent.

Your voice, that was the last thing to go. You can still feel the words, curdling somewhere around the base of your throat, you remember most of them, how it felt to curl your tongue around some of your favourites like *lasciviousness* and *guttural* and *warp coil.*

Warp coil, you say in your mind, popping the P and crackling the hard C.

Another thing you've lost. Star Trek. You used to watch it every day, all the series—even *Enterprise*, which your granddaughter hates. But most of all, the original series, with Kirk and Spock and Uhura and Chekov and Bones and Sulu. And oh, it doesn't matter now, because no one turns on Star Trek for you. Not here.

Your granddaughter showed you how to watch streaming services on a tablet, but you can never remember how to make it work and "Oh honey, you don't want to watch that old crap again," the nurse would say when you could still speak, could still ask her to turn it on for you, when you could still hold it.

"She likes Star Trek," your granddaughter would say on her visits. "It's not hurting anyone."

But it is, you guess. Hurting the other old folks who watch *Jeopardy* and *Wheel of Fortune* and daytime soap operas and shopping channels, even though most of them just stare at the walls or the floor these days, not even looking at the screen.

You met George Takei once, Sulu. Fifty years ago, maybe. Maybe more. Was it sixty? Your shaking hands play over the tablet sitting on the bed at your side and you try to catch the nurse's eye, to somehow implore her to turn on and set up the tablet so you can watch your show. Could you see it one more time? Could you take a ride on the Enterprise once more before you die?

"How'd we get so old?" Edward Collins, the nursing home's class clown, rolls up next to you. He grins and winks, and for a moment, he reminds you of George Takei. The way Sulu winked at you back then, when you saw him at the convention. The way he smiled, so cheekily.

Your granddaughter shows you his videos sometimes—one where he reads from a famous smutty novel and says, "Oh my," and oh, how you'd laughed and laughed. You wish you could see him one more time, just one more time, to tell him how he'd changed your life back then, how you'd been at the lowest point of your life, how Star Trek had saved you again and again. How George had winked at you when you'd cried, had told you that yours was a life worth saving.

You shake your head at Edward but words won't come, they can't come, they never come anymore, just like your kids, like your other grandkids, everyone but Emma who comes every week, sometimes twice, who brings snacks you aren't supposed to eat, who sits on your bed and plays a game–two blinks for the original series, stick out your tongue for *Enterprise*, wink with your right eye for *Deep Space Nine*. Mostly you blink twice even though Emma groans and says, "But it's so outdated, Grandma."

She's twenty now, maybe twenty-one, your Emma. She has a boyfriend, though she hasn't brought him to meet you yet.

"Emma's here," the nurse says and suddenly you're moving, the chair being rolled back to your room and though you want to see Emma, you hate people moving you without warning, hate the sudden loss of equilibrium, the way your stomach flips like you're in freefall, arms pinwheeling in panicked flight but then you're stopped and Emma's face lights up and she's in front of your chair, arms around you and it doesn't matter anymore.

It doesn't matter that you can't speak, that you can't push your own chair. It doesn't matter that you don't know how to turn on the tablet or hold it. It doesn't matter that you can't go to sleep anymore watching Trek.

It only matters that she's here.

"Emma," you mouth, and you're crying but it doesn't bother Emma. She wipes your face and says, "We're going on an outing today, Grandma."

The nurse helps Emma bundle you into a coat and hat and Emma asks if it's okay to move your chair and you manage a nod, though your neck feels weak like it's going to crack if you move your head too much.

She pushes you through the door and the air is cold, but the sun feels lovely on your face and you manage to lift your face to the sky and then Emma is lifting you from your chair to her car and she's so strong, so capable, or have you gotten so thin she barely feels the effort of picking you up?

Her strong hands pull the seatbelt around you. The radio is on. People are talking about Trek.

"It's a podcast," Emma says.

A podcast. Your lips move around the words, though no sound comes out.

"*Women at Warp*," Emma says. "My favourite."

The people are talking about Sulu on *Voyager*. You remember that episode, remember Emma's face when she turned it on for you, her smile as you recognized George Takei, as your brain took in that Sulu (*Sulu!*) was on a newer Trek and all the memories blur as you ride in Emma's car and the women on the podcast talk and you're thinking of George and his words and the wink and Emma is pulling into a crowded parking lot.

She puts a tag in the mirror. Bundles you back into your chair. Pushes past a long line of people.

You wait. Move. Wait. Move. The crowd shifts, jostles, but mostly gives you space. Emma talks to someone at a window. A badge goes around your neck. Emma pushes you through the line and you're almost to the front and the crowd parts.

And then you realize who you're waiting for.

"There he is," Emma says.

You crane your neck to look up at her and she's smiling, crying, and she pushes you to the table and George himself stands to come around and lean down to talk with you, but you can't speak, you can never say what you want to say. "I saw you," you want to tell him but though your mouth moves, nothing comes out.

"She met you," Emma says. "Before I was even born."

You look up at him and the words are so close, it almost hurts and you're crying with frustration because you want to tell him how much he meant to you, how he saved your life, but you're silent, you're always silent.

But George just smiles. And winks. Just like before. His face, older like yours, but that wink, that cheeky wink, how you feel it down to your toes.

And he says, "Oh, yes. Of course I remember."

The Spock 10-Step Method to Surviving a Narcissist

1. **Raise an Eyebrow, Never Your Voice** – Unlike you, Spock doesn't need words to convey judgement. Communicate with the mystery of silence rather than reacting. (Because if you react, he reacts, and you will never regain control.)
2. **Suppress and Survive** – Crying is for humans. You are Vulcan. Tears garner neither sympathy nor concession. He eats tears for breakfast. Are you crying? Why are you crying?
3. **Think Like a Cat** – Slow blink. Stare. Repeat. He's talking about your shortcomings, about the myriad ways in which you've disappointed him, but you're a Vulcan. You do not disappoint. Slow blink. This is next-level disassociation. Be proud.
4. **Never Let Him See the Fear** – A good Vulcan keeps a steady pulse even if they're shaking on the inside. You're imagining things, he says. Don't respond. You're not afraid. You are definitely not afraid.
5. **State the Facts and Refuse to Engage Further** – Spock does not argue. He builds the walls of an argument with bricks of fact. When he asks where you've been, why your grades aren't better, why you are the way you are—state the facts. Go silent while he implodes. Wait for your chance to escape.
6. **Find Your Trusted Person Even If You Can't Unmask** – Even a Vulcan needs their Captain Kirk. Find someone you can confide in, but don't

take the mask all the way off because you can't tell them, you can't tell anyone, everything about your life.

7. **Prepare for the Kobayashi Maru** – Some situations have no winning outcome. You can't win. You cannot win. You can never, ever win. But you don't need to win. You just need it to end.

8. **Bury the Evidence** – Any emotion that surfaces will lead to failure. You don't feel. You don't feel any of this. Crying is for the middle of the night, alone in your room. If you cried at all, which you don't. Don't cry.

9. **Mind Over Matter** – Your body will betray you. It is not you: you are programmed for fight or flight. Your voice will shake, your hands tremble. Your breath will quicken. But you control this. (*No, you don't.* But you must learn using silence and breathing. He wants to devour your weakness, and you must be determined to starve him.)

10. **When All Else Fails, Find Your Own Starship** – As soon as you can, leave. Find your Enterprise. Your crew. A place where emotions don't make you a target but a person. Don't say goodbye or give him a chance to manipulate you into staying.

11. **Bonus Step** – When you deploy number 10, don't look back. Don't you ever, ever look back.

(Don't go back.)

Grab a pen or pencil and finish the next sentence in the space provided below:

I matter because Spock believes I do and also because...

Ortegas's Haircut

Girls should have long hair, my brother says, when Ortegas comes on the bridge during *Strange New Worlds*. His eyes are on the show, but his shoulders, stiff and pointed, crane toward me, toward my fresh buzz cut, maybe my new ink–a rainbow-coloured Starfleet communicator.

My dad grunts behind him in dissent, or maybe it's agreement, I can't tell. The same way he grunted when I told him I wasn't a girl anymore, the same way he grunted when my mom said, *I can't do this anymore*, when she left with a suitcase and a box of unread books she wrote long before my brother and I were born. He never read them, anyway.

My brother stares at the television and, *Girls should have long hair*, he says, the same thing he said when my mother cut off all her own hair, when she got the tattoo, when she put a rainbow sticker on her car, and told us she had something important to talk about and my father grunts again but he looks over at me and, *I love you, Bud*, he says. His big hand rests against the back of my shaved head, just for a second. *I like the haircut,* he says. I don't know if he means mine or Ortegas's, but his hand is heavy and warm on the back of my head and for a moment, I lean into him.

My brother opens his mouth but my father stares him down. *I said I like it*, he repeats, before picking up his beer. My brother's mouth snaps shut. We watch the rest of the show in silence and I've never been happier.

The Mind Meld

My mind to your mind, you say for the second time, and your fingers prod my temples. We stare at each other for a moment, but *I think we have to close our eyes*, you say. We close our eyes, and your fingers press harder and we're silent, but *Maybe your hand is supposed to be further back*, I say, and you readjust your hand. *My mind to your mind.* My eyes are so tightly closed I'm seeing flashes of white spots behind my eyelids and I'm trying to clear my mind, to fall into darkness, to give you a blank slate so we can connect. My legs tingle under me and I want to shift into a more comfortable position, but *Vulcans don't fidget,* you'd chastised when we first decided to try mind melding together, so I focus again on my breathing.

Vulcans can read each other's minds, you had said and *I know*, I'd responded, because I'd seen the episode where Sarek mind melds with Captain Picard, where they share every memory, every thought, and after, they'd connected irrevocably, and when you'd asked me to try to mind meld with you, I'd said yes because maybe if we did, I'd understand why you keep pulling away when I touch you, why you don't come over as often as you used to, why the last time I said I love you, you'd just grunted and picked up the remote.

My mind to your mind, you say again, and the genuine longing in your voice reminds me of the first time you'd asked me on a date. I focus and try and there's nothing, not a glimmer of your thoughts. *I think it's working,* you whisper, and your breath warms my face, while your fingers stroke the hair along my temples. You say it again and I know from your voice that you believe it, that you want to believe it. *My mind to your mind.*

Yes, I say, *I feel it, too.*

There Are No Fat People on Star Trek

There are no fat people on Star Trek, Blondie says, rolling her eyes toward Laney who curls into her corner of the couch and tries to look smaller. Blondie, Dad's third wife, is impeccably slender and perfectly made up. Her lips are probably her plumpest feature and Laney bets she's paid for those.

Blondie and Laney's dad watch Star Trek as a compromise–he goes to events with Blondie, and Blondie sits in front of the television once a week to watch Dad's favourite show. Laney's favourite, too. Laney and her father had made it through Season Two of their second rewatch of *Voyager* before the new arrival, but Blondie, who thinks Captain Janeway is too aggressive, complains throughout.

Laney tries to ignore her, focusing on the show, trying to think of nothing but the story.

But no fat people, Blondie says again. *None.*

Laney's dad says, *That's enough, that's enough*, in a soft voice like he wants to get a point across but he doesn't want to upset Blondie by making it too forcefully.

I'm just stating a fact, Blondie says. *Fatness has been eliminated.*

Laney's father doesn't respond.

Captain Janeway wouldn't hire you, she says, her gaze travelling the plump mounds of fat under Laney's oversize Trek sweatshirt, a men's 2X, the one her dad bought her at the last convention they'd gone to, back before Blondie came into their lives.

Laney can feel Blondie's stare, and she clenches her fists, drawing little half moons on the palms of her hands with her fingernails. She'd draw blood, she would, had she not chewed her fingernails back to their quicks. Because Blondie is right, there really aren't fat people on Star Trek, not really, maybe a few chubby Klingons and maybe that doctor who fell in love with Lwaxana and sure, Scotty got a little portly after he retired, but the only so-called fat Starfleet officer is Tilly, and she isn't even fat, just not as skinny as everyone else.

Laney stares at the TV, her beloved show dying in front of her eyes. She wouldn't exist in the Federation; she wouldn't be welcome. Tears prick her eyes, and she digs her nails deeper into her palms because she'd rather hurt physically than emotionally.

It isn't that there are no fat people in Star Trek, Laney's father says. His hand falls heavily on Laney's arm and he gives her a quick smile. *It's that there's no fat-shaming.*

Blondie opens her mouth, but for once, Laney's father talks over her. *There's no fat-shaming on Star Trek*, he repeats. *And there's none in this house.*

He gives Laney's arm a squeeze and another smile. *And I need Star Trek and I need you*, he says, and his voice is so strong, so sure. *Captain Janeway would love you.* She almost wants to believe him.

Almost.

Later that night, after Laney's dad and Blondie have gone to bed, Laney stares at her laptop, *Voyager* playing on her tablet beside her.

She scrolls pictures of Janeway, Seven of Nine, Tuvok. All strong. All slender. She types, 'Body positivity in Star Trek' into the search bar.

The first article to pop up is "Why There Are No Fat People in Starfleet."

Laney clicks and reads, but the words don't help. Replicators, easy access to healthcare, the ability to exactly control caloric intake with nutrients, a society free from fatphobia not because the society has evolved to be better than that, but because it has evolved to weed out fatness.

In other words, in Starfleet, Laney wouldn't be herself.

She closes the tab. She doesn't want proof that she wouldn't exist in Starfleet. She gets enough of that from Blondie, from the world, from herself even.

She scrolls through Tumblr instead, listening to Voyager in the background, an episode where Neelix fucks up by accidentally running drugs from a space station and Janeway is so pissed but doesn't kick him off the ship, because he's part of their family.

Laney clicks on a post called "Fat Trek" and there she is. Not her, not exactly but so many fat Trek characters like plus-size Vulcans and a fat Uhura and chubby Kirk and the entire Voyager crew, and she's in the rabbit hole of something she never realized even existed. Laney exhales, near tears.

She opens another image. A picture of a fan, a fat fan, a girl as big as Laney, maybe bigger. And she's at a convention with Kate Mulgrew, Janeway, and Kate's got her arms around the girl and they're both smiling, hugging and smiling, and the girl has tears in her eyes.

Laney reblogs the post and pulls her tablet over to watch the rest of the Voyager episode. Because she realizes her dad is right. Janeway would love her. And if Janeway could love her, Laney could love herself.

The Prodigy

I hate him, I'd told my mom before leaving the house that day. But I don't hate my dad. Not really. But if I could swap him for a normal dad, one who doesn't miss weekends with me so he can fly to California and dress up as a Starfleet captain, I'd definitely consider it.

Maybe someone like Tom's dad who comes to all the baseball games, or even my mom's new boyfriend Alan, who keeps buying me pizza and calling me Sport. Hawaiian pizza. "Betcha never had anything this good, eh, Sport?" Gross.

Dad is only ten minutes late this time, which might be a new record of timeliness for him. It's so embarrassing—his car is covered with the most ridiculous bumper stickers. *I Brake for Tribbles* and *Make It So.*

He gives me a half hug when I get in the car and he's raving about the convention, how he'd wished I could have been there, and telling me we're going to watch *Prodigy* when we get home.

"You're going to love it," he says as he drives to his apartment, the crappy one-and-a-half-bedroom walk-down, where my room is about the size of the closet in my bedroom at home.

But I'm not gonna love it. I'm not even going to like it. "I don't like Star Trek," I snap, slouching in my seat. A little pit of guilt settles in my stomach at the hurt look on his face, but I punch it down. He deserves to hurt.

"You used to love Star Trek," he says.

"Yeah, when I was like six."

The thing is, I don't even hate Star Trek. I just hate that he cares about it more than me, how he talks about it all the time, how he acts as if Jake Sisko is really his kid, or how he's so proud of Wesley for figuring out the nanobot thing. How he just gave up our weekend so he could go to a Star Trek thing, how he just texted me to say he'd see me the following weekend. A text. Not even a phone call.

The car is silent except Dad's fingers tapping on the steering wheel. I know he's nervous and for a minute, I want to try to make up, but I can't think of what to say. And anyway, what would it matter? We're friends again until the next important thing comes up? Until he misses my next game?

He finally reaches around into the backseat, digging in the messy pile of uniform jackets, a lanyard, and something I'm pretty sure is a stuffed tribble. He pulls out a T-shirt and hands it to me. "It's a Prodigy T-shirt," he says, smiling hopefully.

The colours are kind of cool, but I don't know. I've never even seen the show. It's a kids' show. I'm twelve, not six. "Why?"

"Dal, the main character, reminds me of you, a little," Dad says. "A lot, really."

"You missed last weekend." I don't want to talk about it, but I can't keep from saying it, from telling him how he'd hurt me, how I'd wanted him to come, how I had to play catch in the backyard with Alan instead.

"I'm sorry."

Ugh. He always says that. Usually, I say it's okay but not this time. He's always sorry for something.

For missing my games. For leaving me and Mom in the first place.

"It was the biggest convention, and I was invited to be a panellist . . ." Whatever, Dad. I stare out the window, clamping my lips together because I want to scream at him. Who cares about being a panellist? What's more important than your own kid? The panel was probably stupid as hell.

"Hey Bud," he says. "You with me?"

"No." My mom would say I'm being a super brat right now, but I don't care.

"I don't fit in most places," he says. "Not with your mom. Not at work. Not even with you, sometimes, though I love you so much."

I keep staring out the window, even though I kind of want to hold his hand like I'm a kid again.

He's still talking. "I try, though. Being normal. Being a better dad. Being more like Alan."

"Don't be like Alan," I say.

"He's a good man," Dad replies. "And he's good for your mom. And you."

Mom likes Alan a lot. I hate his cheerful voice. My dad's voice is deep and comforting.

"When I go to conventions, I don't feel like a jerk," Dad says. "Everyone is a nerd. Even the ones who aren't, if you know what I mean." He taps the comm badge on his T-shirt. "It's like, people really like me. For me."

"You love your Star Trek friends more than me."

"Whoa whoa whoa whoa whoa. No way!" Dad's hands grip the wheel as he swings into the parking lot of his apartment complex. He jams on the brakes before finding a spot. "I love Trek, yes, but what I love most is when the characters remind me of you. Wesley's intelligence. And Dal's disregard for the rules." He grins. "Jake's insight and his questionable fashion choices." He pauses and looks at me as if he's really seeing me, like maybe I'm more than just some jerk, like maybe he likes me for me. He touches my shoulder. "You're the best of the lot, kid. The best kid I've ever had."

"Har, har," I say, because I'm his only kid, but my heart is beating wildly, and I want to believe him.

We sit in the car for a while, Dad tapping the wheel as always, like something has to move even when he's sitting still. I want to tell him that I don't always belong, either. That the guys hang out with each other after games and I'm never invited. That everyone at school has a BFF except me. That when Alan claps me on the shoulder and calls me Sport, it makes me want to puke right in his face.

"Dad," I say, and he turns to look at me, giving me his full attention. "Next time you go, can I come with you?"

The smile explodes onto his face and for the first time today, maybe for the first time in months, he looks . . . well, he looks happy. "It's a deal, Luc." He uses my name. Luc.

We go inside and he asks what I want to do. Maybe I want to play ball, I think. But maybe. Maybe *Prodigy* won't be so bad. "Let's watch some Prodigy," I tell him. "I'll wear my new T-shirt."

Dad opens his mouth to say something—probably something dorky about warp speed—but then he stops and looks at me like he's thinking about it.

Then he says, "Why don't we go play some ball, and watch Trek after?"

He's choosing me first. His arm goes around me and he's solid and he's real, and he's here, and at least for right now, we're connected.

"And then maybe we can get some pizza?" he says.

"No Hawaiian though, please?"

"Hawaiian," he says. "Who would eat Hawaiian? That's just gross."

You Probably Don't

You probably don't know this, but this is the only place I truly feel safe. Here with my wife and my cat and my space heater and my comfortable chair, where I'm not outside dealing with looks, with strangers, with taking too much space, with snap judgements people make the moment they see me, with misgendering, misnaming, body-shaming, and not just from them but from myself.

At home, watching *Star Trek Discovery* where Adira is non-binary and Stamets and Dr. Culber are a gay couple, where women casually mention their wives, where no one says Tilly should lose weight, where people look different, sound different, act different.

And you can't always tell, but this is the reason I often say no when you invite me to your parties. Why should I come when I can be home where no one ever says, *I respect your pronouns, but they/them is plural, so I'm going to call you entity instead.*

And you can't know this, but my wife and I overplan before we come to your events, whether it's okay to hold hands, whether we should introduce ourselves as a married couple, whether I should tell you my pronouns, or let you assume I'm someone I'm not.

And we come home after and escape into another binge watch of *Discovery* where the only response to Adira's proclamation—*my pronouns are they/them*—is a smile and loving acceptance. We study Stamets's face like we study yours, but on his, we only see acceptance.

In real life, we study you for safety, for smiles, for an indication you're not a danger to us before we let you see who we really are, other than who you think you want us to be.

Don't overthink it. And we'll stop overplanning.

For the One Who Didn't Make Captain

STARFLEET CASUALTY REPORT

Name:[Redacted]
Rank: Cadet
Assignment: N/A
Cause of Death:[Redacted]

Commander's Summary:

Cadet 8653 ~~(fuck, I wish I'd used their name more)~~was ~~one of those kids~~a promising cadet ~~who could navigate the warp core with greater ease than a social gathering~~with an encyclopedic knowledge of Starfleet history, regulations, and warp field dynamics. They could recite warp field equations with startling accuracy. ~~And often did. Usually while I was trying to drink coffee in silence.~~ They demonstrated a relentless commitment to the ideals of the Federation and a steadfast belief that every crew member matters. ~~Annoyingly earnest and painfully anxious and way too familiar to a certain admiral who used to believe in idealism more than procedure.~~

On Stardate 5869.1, the cadet arrived for breakfast with newly dyed purple hair and ~~said they were rocking the Boim~~cited Bradward Boimler as an inspiration. ~~Not gonna lie, it looked fucking incredible.~~The deceased frequently expressed admiration for Lt. Bradward Boimler, a Starfleet

Officer, citing his unwavering belief that even a basket case could make captain someday. Deceased once told me they felt as if they were on the "Lower Decks" of life. ~~I thought it was a joke. I shouldn't have laughed.~~

Incident Report:

~~Cadet 8653 submitted logs that were specific enough to make me uncomfortable. Pages of observations, complete with footnotes and citations, outlining the ways in which we could do better. We should have done better.~~Despite possessing intellectual brilliance and a deep passion for exploration, the deceased struggled with feelings of insignificance. They were known for submitting detailed logs regarding their observations with no official response ever recorded.

The deceased was found in their personal quarters on Stardate 5873.4. No distress calls recorded. No sign of a struggle.~~ Except there were signs, weren't there? I saw them—we all saw them. Quirks, some of us said, shrugging them off with awkward laughs.~~

Personal logs indicate bullying, but the administration has uncovered no concrete proof of any substantiating facts. School officials deny culpability.~~The bullying. Why the fuck didn't I fully investigate harder?~~

Final Log Entry Recovered From Personal Device:

If I lived on the Lower Decks, I wouldn't be so weird. I mean, maybe I would, but I wouldn't be the only weird one. Hell, I probably wouldn't even be the weirdest. After all, Boimler is a wreck and Mariner tried to beat up her own mom, and Tendi and Rutherford have the most ridiculous platonic love relationship and also Ransom with his working out and just all of it. I don't even think I'd stand out if I lived in the Lower Decks, not even with dyed hair because hello, Boimler! And he has friends! Mariner, Tendi, Rutherford love him the way he is, just the way he is, even when he screws everything up because he's overthinking everything. They even forgave him for fucking up buffer time. He has it all and I have shit. Maybe in a mirror universe, I'll have a crew.

Command Recommendation:

~~Protocol requires me to state that~~Cadet acted of their own accord. No official reprimands warranted.

~~Protocol can fuck itself.~~

Personal Note:

Cadet often inserted obscure, oddly specific *Star Trek* references into conversations and I wish I'd laughed more than I rolled my eyes. I wish I'd taken five minutes to understand, to welcome them into my own weird niche obsessions, to show them that sometimes, having just one person who understands can make the entire universe seem less hostile. I failed them. We all failed them.

Computer, redact personal note. Redact all of it.

[Computer: *Redaction request denied.*]

Laken, Like the Water

I'm Laken, they tell me, pointing to their nametag. *Lake, like the water.*

We're sitting on a bench outside the conference center. I'd been standing in line to see the cast of *Discovery*, something I'd paid more than I could afford to do, but my feet hurt, and the crowd gave me a panic attack, and now here's this person trying to talk to me, so I drop a *that's nice* in their direction, and keep my eyes focused on the ducks. The bench was empty when I sat down, and now it is not. Someone has taken the other half of the bench. Someone who is talkative.

Who's your favourite captain? Laken says. They're wearing the vest uniform Picard wore in the *First Contact* movie and I have to admit they wear it well. So when they smile at me my mouth twitches at the corner but I tap my foot and cross my arms trying to give the impression that I'm not someone who wants to make small talk, even though their eyebrow does this cute lifting thing when they smile and I'm half tempted to ask them if anyone has ever told them they kind of look like Spock—sexy young Ethan Peck Spock, not Leonard Nimoy Spock, though he was sexy too, if you ask me.

Janeway, I say, though really, I don't have a favourite and I love Sisco and Picard and Berman and not Archer, but it's all too much to say and I don't want to get drawn into a conversation but Laken says, *I can never pick a favourite—I love them all.*

Even Archer? I say.

Especially Archer, they respond and I can't help but laugh and, for a moment, the angry bees buzzing in my stomach settle.

I was supposed to be with the cast of Discovery, I say, and Laken says, *Me too.*

Then why are you out here?

I saw you run away and worried you were ill.

I want to think they're a weirdo, stalking me, and checking on me, but something in the set of their shoulders spells safety and the galaxies in their eyes somehow say *come with me* and when they hold out a hand and ask me to go back in and see if we can still make the event, my hand slips into theirs and before I can stop myself, I'm standing and smiling. *Make it so*, I say, and Laken does.

Don't Shut Up, Wesley

We're watching *Next Gen*, my mom and my dad and me and my older brother, golden brother, Tom, who won a football scholarship and who is wearing my dad's number this year and *aren't they gorgeous*, my mom always says, when they put their arms around each other and pose for big burly men pictures.

Tom says something about ten-yard lines or cheerleaders or a new part he needs for his car and my parents stare at him like he's the second coming of Christ, for shit's sake. "That's so interesting, Tom," my mother says over and over. "Great job, son," my dad says.

We're watching *Next Gen*, but really I'm watching it, and they just happen to be in the room, sitting at the small table behind the couch where my parents play cards and Tom sits with them because he has a date later and he's probably going to ask my dad for money. He doesn't have to ask to borrow the car because he has his own. My dad bought it for his sixteenth birthday.

I'm trying to ignore them all because it's a Wesley episode, the one where Lore comes back and pretends to be Data and everyone believes him except Wesley and when Wesley tries to tell the adults what's going on, Captain Picard says, "Shut up, Wesley."

But Wesley Crusher, as usual, is the only person who knows what's going on and no one listens to him because he's just some nerdy kid, just like me, and here's Captain Picard, my hero, my substitute dad, the man who saves us all, all the time, saying, "Shut up, Wesley."

Wesley tries to defend himself, but he's shut down again. This time by his mother. "Shut up, Wesley," she says.

Wesley is hurt. You can see it in his face. I want to hug him. The grown-ups move on. I'm clenching my hands at the injustice of it all. Golden boy Tom doesn't even notice. Brothers suck. If Wesley had a brother, they'd probably all listen to him.

And I sit there, the weight of it settling in my chest like I've been kicked by the goal-kicker or whatever the hell the guy is on Tom's football team. *Shut up, Wesley.*

But it's worse when my dad mutters, "That kid's annoying."

I don't know if he's talking about Wesley or me. But I pretend we're talking about the show.

"He's the only one who knows Lore is trying to get them killed," I say, but Tom says, "Shut up, Evan."

"Not nice, Tom," my mother says, but there's amusement in her voice.

"Sorry, sorry," Tom says, but he's not sorry, not at all.

Shut up, Evan, follows me to bed, to school. How funny for everyone. How funny for the audience. Shut up, Wesley. Shut up, Evan.

It follows me to third period English where I sit in my assigned seat next to Gina Hadley who doesn't talk to me. To be fair, she doesn't talk to anyone, not even our teacher who calls on her sometimes, pausing with disdain on her face at Gina's continued silence, before moving on to someone else.

Chad and Trent, two freshmen on the team with my brother, sit behind me singing the Star Trek theme.

"Tom says Evan loves Westley," Chad says.

"Ewwww," Trent replies. "Evan is gay for Westley."

I want to scream at them, to toss my books at them. Or explain to them that my love for Wesley isn't because I'm gay, it's because Wesley speaks his mind even when adults tell him to shut up. Wesley solves the problems even when no one listens. Wesley keeps trying even when he's shut down again and again.

Next to me, Gina shifts as the boys continue their attack.

"Evan loves Westley," they chant together and then one of them pokes me in the back and I whirl around but before I can open my mouth, Gina whirls around too.

"His name is Wesley," she snaps at Chad, whose mouth drops open. "It's not Westley."

Trent stares at her. "We didn't–"

"Shut up, Trent," Gina says.

As Gina and I turn back to face the front of the room, she smiles. She leans over and whispers in my ear, "Do you want to come over and watch Star Trek?"

For a moment, something unclenches in my chest. I don't know what to say, what to do, but she looks at me, and I can't see any sign of mockery in her eyes. The idea of watching Trek, actually watching Trek, with someone who loves the show, makes me want to scream or cry. Or both.

"I'll bring popcorn," I tell her.

"Just bring yourself," she says. "I've got you covered."

Beam Me Up, Cat

The cat beams into our apartment unexpectedly. Or rather, it is just sitting there on the window ledge when I get out of the shower. The window is closed. Did I let it in?

I swear this to my wife Sophie when she comes into the bedroom holding a half-eaten bagel, which is as strange to me as a cat in our window, but she doesn't believe me. "Where'd it come from, Janey?" she asks, biting into the bagel instead of ripping it the way I like to.

"Honestly," I tell her. "It was just there."

"We said we weren't adopting another cat," she says before turning to continue getting ready to go to work. "Take it back to wherever it came from."

"I'm sure the cat would like to go back to its home, too," I say.

"Funny," she says. "Wherever you got it, take it back."

She glowers at me and I don't offer a defense. But where the hell does she think I found a cat at seven o'clock in the morning?

I hear the front door slam as she leaves angrily. I can't blame her. My heart isn't ready for another four-legged monster either, not after losing Odo, the long-haired rescue who stole our hearts, gave us ten years, and died suddenly of an incurable disease. I still remember holding his little paw, watching Sophie's tears, feeling helpless to comfort either of them through my own grief.

"Why can't cats live forever?" I ask this new cat who has paraded into my house, slow-blinking back like Spock staring at someone having a nervous breakdown, as if to say, *I'm here now. Make the most of it.*

But it's going back. Back to wherever it came from. "Where did you come from?" I ask, though the cat doesn't answer. They never answer, not when they don't want to. It follows me through the house as I check all the doors and windows to make sure they are closed tight. Maybe it did beam itself into my life. I'm torn between ushering it out the door and calling someone to come get it. But who?

My wife sends me a text with a bunch of question marks and a frowning emoji.

I'm working on it, I text back and she doesn't answer. I know what she'll say if she comes home and it's still here.

"We work too much," she'll say. "You travel too much."

It's all true and yet the cat crawls into my lap when I sit to watch an episode of *Prodigy*, and it follows me into my office when I go to slam out another freelance article—something I do to pay the bills while writing my ultimate science fiction epic.

The cat manages to knock everything off my desk, jump to the windowsill in my office, knock over my spider plant, bend three slats on the blind, and rush into the kitchen, presumably looking for a place to pee.

?????, my wife texts.

Still trying, I write back.

And I am trying. But where do you take someone who just appears in your house? The shelter? The cat watches me from the floor, its marmalade-and-cream-coloured face, its unusually large ears, the fluffy tufts of orange hair between its toes.

"God, but you're cute," I say, as I contemplate my options. I imagine Odo, the cat, not the shape-shifter, and his soulful eyes. "What would Odo do?" I mutter aloud. But I know what he would do. Odo the cat and Odo the character would go to the store for food and a litter box, so I do.

When I come home, laden with the detritus of cat ownership, the cat is asleep in my wife's chair and I've missed three texts while I was driving, texts I didn't bother looking at because I know they'll all be some variation on the question of whether or not I've gotten rid of it.

I toss the new cat toys into the air, but the cat ignores them. By the time I unload the cat stuff, put food in a bowl and fill a water dish, the cat is tearing through the living room, batting around my wife's *Next Generation* comm badge. Great.

"Listen," I tell it. "You're going to have to behave."

The cat bats the comm badge under the TV and disappears in an instant. I search for the cat until I find the fucker in my wife's office, her Spock figurine in its little mouth.

"I'm home," my wife calls from the living room. "And that cat better . . ."

Her words pause with her footsteps. I know what's next. A sigh. A deep, weary sigh of exhaustion, inevitability, and the realization that whatever happens next is going to be a battle she's probably already lost.

"You didn't get rid of it," she says flatly, because, clearly, I haven't.

"I tried."

She doesn't speak for a long moment and I'm aware that I'm holding my breath. The cat is gone, out of the office, and I hear the sound of a cat toy skittering across the hardwood floor and then my wife flopping onto the couch. I tiptoe to the door and peer around the corner. My wife stares at the cat who has perched on the arm of the couch next to her. They stare at each other for long moments without blinking until my wife closes her eyes and sighs again. The cat slips off the arm of the couch, into her lap and maybe she doesn't even realize it, but she's petting it, rubbing her hand over its little furry head and the cat is purring like it's finally come home after years of being lost.

And hope flares in my chest, hope for her, hope for me, hope for our shared grief, hope for the love of a new cat, and hope that tomorrow we won't see a *Missing Cat* poster stapled to the telephone poles. I crawl onto the couch next to them and my wife puts one arm around me, other hand still petting the cat.

"Well?" I say in a whisper, barely daring to speak.

"Does he have a name?" she says.

"I was hoping you would have one."

"What do you think about Quark?" she says.

"Quark?" I say, and the cat chirps, staring into my eyes. I swear it gives a small nod. Resistance, for her, for me, for us all, was clearly futile. "Quark it is."

Ten Forward. 3 a.m.

The diner is pretty much empty. The server, a bored-looking old guy in an apron, brought our drinks and plates of eggs and pancakes and left a giant carafe of coffee before disappearing into the kitchen.

There's a couple guys in high-vis sitting at the counter. Miners, maybe, or construction crew, just getting off a late shift.

And also, the Cool Person. Gender indeterminate, coolness level ridiculous. The kind of cool that irritates me, that kind of effortless cool that radiates the fact they'd probably slam me into a locker if we were all still in high school. Shaggy hair, cheekbones for days, and absolutely devastating lips, and they keep looking at our table like we're a particularly interesting zoo exhibit. *What the hell do they even want?*

They are, without a doubt, judging us. Judging me. And to be fair, we're worthy of judging since our table is currently in a shouting match over our favourite and least favourite parts of Trek.

"I'm just saying." Maddy waves her fork around so bits of scrambled egg fly across the table like the Delta Flyer in a space race. "Seven of Nine dated Chakotay because he's so boring she knew it would be safe."

"Like a beta test?" Jamie says around a mouthful of toast, the words rolling out while the toast stays in.

"She needed to prove to herself that she could date someone. Testing her humanity, so to speak."

She uses her fork like a rake to keep the eggs from touching the baked beans. "Chakotay was like, the most basic person she could find."

I'm distracted by the Cool Person who keeps looking at us inbetween sips of their stupidly tiny cup of espresso. And who drinks espresso at 3 a.m., anyway? Cool people. That's who. Screw them. I'm with my crew, my family. I'm safe. "I still think Seven and B'lanna would have made a better couple than either of them made with their wishy-washy men."

"I'll concur that Chakotay is the human equivalent of a dentist office motivational poster," Jamie says. "But Tom wasn't wishy-washy."

"Irritating, yes," Brodie adds. "Wishy-washy, no."

"What does wishy-washy even mean?" I say, not looking at them, but at the Cool Person.

The Cool Person's mouth twitches, but they're staring at a book now and I have to resist the urge to crane my neck to see what it is. Probably some obscure poetry or . . . oh, who knows? What do cool people read? *How To Destroy a Nerd In 10 Easy Steps?*

"Lwaxana Troi," Jamie says, slamming their hand down on the table. "The most layered, complex, engaging character in all of Trek."

"The episode where she and Alex are in the mud bath," Maddy says. She sighs.

"The higher, the fewer," Jamie says in the deepest octave they can muster.

Hammy, who'd been shovelling hash browns on to his fork and then into his mouth through most of the conversation, looks up from his plate. "Her thing with Odo, though. Pushy."

"Hello?" I yank my gaze from the Cool Person's table to stare down Hammy. "Her thing with bucket-man was nothing but perfection." Hammy opens his mouth, but I stare him down. "Nothing. But. Perfection."

"When she takes off the wig to give him a place to ooze," Maddy says, and now Brodie sighs.

The Cool Person is smirking. Smirking! They're not looking up, but they are smirking, and I know they're taking field notes to regale all their cool friends later. A study of nerds in the wild. They could do a fucking podcast on it. They are probably going to order another cup of tiny espresso so they can sit here and hear some more.

"Riker and Ransom having an affair," Jamie says. "The crossover episode we need!"

"More queer Trek," Brodie shouts and everyone cheers. Everyone except me. I can't stop glancing to the next table where Coolio is currently pretending not to look at us.

I don't care. I don't. It took me years to find my group. Years of loneliness, of sitting in my room alone, of haunting social media groups to find my around-the-world folks. Having this family, this group. It's my life. And I'm not letting some judgy jerkoff ruin my enjoyment of this moment.

"Anyway," Brodie says. "Can we please talk about the evolution of Worf?"

"I love him," Jamie says. "But I'm gonna say it. He's a jerk in DS9."

The Cool Person looks up sharply. Our eyes meet and I quickly look away, sure a blush is creeping up my face. Why am I like this? "Look,

Worf's a jerk in DS9 because all this shit happened in TNG and people would just like die horribly and the next episode, he was just back at work pretending nothing happened."

"No one processed crap in TNG," Maddy says.

"Fair," Jamie adds.

Hammy swallows another bite of breakfast. "Also just going to say this. Wesley's thing with the Traveler was the Star Trek version of joining a timey-wimey space polycule."

"SHUT UP!" Ava flings a hashbrown off a fork toward Hammy's forehead. "You think everything is a space polycule."

"I mean, Garek, O'Brien, Keiko, and Julian," I say.

"Okay, but . . ." Ava laughs and then we're all laughing.

I shouldn't care what a random stranger thinks. This is my life, my dream. My family. How I'd longed for them all my life and now that we're here, I can't imagine a life without them. And yet, I can't fully focus on the debate because I can feel that stupid Cool Person staring at me like I'm a social experiment unfolding before their eyes and it shouldn't bother me, but it does. My family is not someone's late night entertainment, and we should be able to have a heated discussion in a mostly empty diner without some judgemental jerk using us as mockery fodder.

I can't take it another minute.

"What?!" I shout, locking eyes with the Cool Person, glaring with the full weight of all the rage I can muster. "May I help you? Do you need something? Would you like me to summon Apron Man to bring you something?"

We stare at each other for a long moment. My friends have gone completely silent. And I'm waiting. Waiting for the Cool Person to tell the nerds to get a life, or to shut up and let them enjoy their coffee in peace.

Instead, they cock an eyebrow, half smile on those devastating lips and I swear to god they nearly wink at me. That smirk. I'm devastated. Broken. "Odo is basically naked," they say. "All the time."

Everyone loses it like they have just heard the punchline to a joke they've been waiting for all their lives. Hammy spits scrambled eggs. Maddy screams into her hands. Brodie and Jamie erupt with "Ewwwww!" in unison.

And me. I've forgotten how to breathe in this liminal space between astonishment and the fucking funniest thing I've ever heard anywhere, let alone a dingy diner on First Street at 3 a.m. when nothing is supposed to make sense.

But they're right. Odo's uniform is part of his body. He's naked.

All the time.

"So," I say, looking at the Cool Person straight between their devastating lips, "where do you think his comm badge goes when he turns into goo?"

The Cool Person grins. "This is a point worthy of debate"—they raise their hands in a half-shrug—"with someone other than myself."

"That's what the diner is for," I say.

"That's what friends are for," the Cool Person answers, and I realize, under that smirk, they might possibly look a little lonely.

"Please join us," I say, and Maddie says, "Yes, please!"

"Seriously?" they ask.

"Seriously," Hammy says, hashbrown bits flying out of his mouth.

We all shift over to make room.

"Join us," I repeat. And they do.

The old guy with the apron brings out a second carafe of coffee, like he always does, and seeing the Cool Person now sitting at our table, walks back to the kitchen with the same bored look he walked out with, to get another cup of espresso.

Teddy at the Convention

We watch them bustle in—people in plain clothes, folks in costume. We admire the homemade costumes, the mashups, the people dressed in Starfleet uniforms with Darth Vader masks. We love them all, we don't tell them this, but we do.

We see them strolling together—a father and his child—and we don't know why they catch our eye, this pair out of the hundreds or the thousands of people, why they stand out, what draws us to them. Maybe the way the child stares up at her dad or the way her tiny fingers clutch what looks like a mid-70s Spock doll or maybe we just saw something in the dad's eyes, something lost, something searching for a home, but we watch them, this parent-and-child Vulcan pair and we know them.

They hold hands as they stand in line, and when the child tires, the father picks her up and holds her against his shoulder, and when they finally get to the front of the line, the man says, "Star Trek saved my life," and we know it, it's saved ours too, but there's something in his eyes and when he says, "My name is Teddy and this is my daughter, Trina," we say, "Welcome home, Teddy."

New Life and New Civilizations

We are the Bridge Crew. We found each other in dorm rooms, at comic-cons, in the back rows of bad queer movies, where we whispered our wished-for endings to each other. We connected in hostels, in homeless shelters, in the basement of someone's parents' house after our own parents kicked us out. We recognized each other in the wild—with a rainbow pin, a shy glance, in the way someone's shoulders eased when they realized they weren't alone.

We learned each other's real names—the ones we whispered to ourselves in the mirror before we had the courage to say them out loud. The names that weren't given to us, but the ones we claimed. We heard our names from each other's mouths and we became real.

We are the Bridge Crew. We are each the captain, taking turns leading the rest. Who's at the helm? Who's charting the course, guiding us away from trouble, from the cops outside the bar, from the fists that come for us when we leave the safety of our numbers? We command each other, take each other's orders, knowing we'll always answer the call.

We are each other's first officer too. We stand behind the captain, take the hard jobs, act as liaison to the others. We're a friend, sometimes, empathetic and approachable, the one people want to be around. We navigate the endless rules, the unjust legislation, the oppressive politicians.

We are each the doctor. We care for one another's scars, inside and out. We stitch up the broken places, hold each other steady when the world tilts sideways. We press our mouths to each other's skin and breathe into the wounds.

We are each the communications officer. We listen when no one else will, we stand in for each other's parents and guardians. We learn the new ways because the old ones didn't serve us, because we didn't grow up knowing how to talk without yelling or cowering. But we do now.

We are each the head of security. We stand between their world and our own. We don't flinch. We take the hits, and we fight back. When someone comes for one of us, they come for all of us. The center holds, we say. We are the center. When one of us is beaten in the streets, when another spends a night in jail because they dared fight back, we find the ones who hurt the crew. We show them the airlock.

We are the Bridge Crew. We are found family, stitched together from love, guilt, fear and scars, from laughter and late-night rescues. We are each other.

And we are home.

Acknowledgements

If I forget a name, please forgive me. I was watching Star Trek while writing this—the one where Data builds a daughter, teaches her about love, and then loses her. All I could think about afterward was how deeply wondrous it is that an android doesn't technically have feelings and yet somehow inspires so many in the rest of us. Maybe like some of the stories in this book.

That said, there are a few people who cannot be forgotten when it comes to this book.

First, Andy Shaughnessy who beta read when it was in draft form and didn't make fun of me no matter how long my sentences got (and we both know they got long).

My wife August, who endured months of me wandering the house mumbling about which series to include, which characters deserved their own stories, and whether something was missing in the overall arc. Being married to a writer has its perks.

My bestie, Andrew Buckley, who is not a Trekkie, but who redeems his good taste by loving my writing (and me) nonetheless.

Miranda Krogstad, who's pun-fluence was in my head the entire time I was writing "Make it Soap."

The folks at Pulp Literature who not only publish my stories, but who also make up part of my found family. You make this slog less lonely.

Marion Lougheed, friend, editor, champion of weird little books, and extraordinary human being who keeps saying "yes" to my novellas-in-flash.

Bonus Content

The following stories are from *Ravens Don't Get High Blood Pressure and other tales of queer love* by Finnian Burnett, forthcoming.

A Moon More Beautiful

Chloe skids the jeep to the side of the road and stops at the edge of a field, near a wood fence. Without streetlights or the welcoming beacons from suburban front porches, the moon is the brightest light. It hangs, low and full, ripe with possibilities, like us before we moved in together. *Us* before I learned she doesn't speak during meals and doesn't want to hear my voice, either. *Us* before she discovered I snore and cough in my sleep. *Us* before *you flirt too much* and *but I did the dishes yesterday.*

Us before *whose dirty socks are on the floor?* and *who was the last one to clean the kitty litter?*

We step out of the jeep and holding hands, walk to the fence. I kick a rock and stumble, flailing for a moment for my next step. She steadies me automatically, her grip firm and sure in my hand. Even under the full moon, the fields are dark and long shadows sway with the trees. A chill in the wind sends goosebumps up my arms and I pull my coat tighter.

I wonder if she's brought me out here to kill me, or if maybe she plans to get me onto the fence and sprint for the jeep, leaving me out here with the coyotes. She's thinner than I am, sportier. She could make it to the jeep before I managed to get one leg back over the fence.

At home, she'll drink a beer, grateful that she'll never again toss and turn to the sound of my snoring and coughing. She'll eat a meal, every meal, in peace and silence. Or maybe she'll stare out the window at the full moon, remembering the softness of my hands or the time we stripped on a beach in Michigan and ran, laughing and screaming, into the lake in November.

Her hands are strong as she helps me climb to the top of the fence. Strong like they were at my waist the first time we danced and steady as they were when she first brushed a piece of hair from my face. I can't see her face in the darkness and I don't know if she's thinking about the moon, or about me. Maybe she's thinking about the last time I said I love you or maybe she's wondering if she loves my possibilities more than she loves me.

"Sitting here almost makes you forget everything else," she says, giving my hand a squeeze.

Everything else is the fight we had in the jeep on the way home from the party and she's right. The moon is so beautiful, it almost makes me forget how tightly her hands gripped the steering wheel, how her lips pressed together in anger when I said I was tired of her policing my conversations with people. "Flirtations, you mean," she had said in a dark voice. "Your flirtations with people."

And how in the silence after, I'd stared out the window and convinced myself to leave. To just pack up when we got home and walk out. How I'd finally come to believe that I'd be better off alone than with her until she screeched off the road in the middle of nowhere to bring me to this fence and stare at this beautiful moon and now, sitting here holding her hand, it seems like our love has been filled with more moments like this and fewer moments like that.

"The moon is beautiful tonight," she says.

"It is."

We perch there, holding hands, staring at the moon. And the moon is beautiful and full of possibilities, even when we are not.

Lift Capacity

Elevator three, the sign says, the only elevator in the building that goes to every floor, but Sian knows he won't go beyond the eighth floor, won't press the number twelve, won't knock on Theo's door, touch his soft hands, ask for one more chance.

Elevator three. Sian runs his fingers over the grimy wall, the grooves of the brick rough under his fingers. Behind him, the parking garage is quiet, folks are home for the evening—this is a quiet building, mostly middle-aged professionals who spend their off-time keeping to themselves in their individual boxes. Sian was the only outlier, fresh out of a relationship and lonely. He needed friends, people to distract him from the endless long evenings of binge-watching *Corner Gas* with his cat. Sian would never love again, but at least he could make friends. He started a community social hour, got permission from the landlord to plant a shared garden on the roof, and put up a barter board in the lobby for neighbours to post items or services for trade.

Willing to dog sit, the first note had said, and Sian had called the number, talked to a man named Theo, and had eventually gone to apartment 1201 where Theo said he was home on disability and looking for stress-free ways to fill his days. He asked about the dog and Sian had to admit he had a cat and was worried it was getting lonely during the day when Sian was at work.

I'm not much of a cat person, Theo said, *but I'm willing to check in on the little guy.*

Sian offered to pay.

But it's a barter board, Theo insisted, and the only thing Sian could offer was food. They exchanged keys and Theo would come down to the eighth floor to sit with Bucky during the day and in the evenings, Sian would cook for Theo. Theo's apartment had the better view, but Sian's kitchen was built for cooking. Sian found out Theo loved Vonnegut and sweet and sour chicken.

Sian told Theo about the time he wet his pants in third grade and everyone called him Betty Wetty for two years. Theo talked about losing his mother before he was old enough to realize how much she loved him. Then, at some point, maybe weeks or months later, they sat on the couch and laughed over something, laughed until Theo was crying and Sian touched Theo's face and kissed him. After that, it was like they'd always been lovers.

Theo wanted to move in, but Sian held him off. He didn't trust Theo not to break his heart. He watched Theo play with Bucky, watched the way the cat curled against Theo's side when he sat on the floor playing video games, how Theo's hand would occasionally drop to Bucky's side and pet the soft fur. Sian would shutter his heart and remind himself he was not falling in love, he would never fall in love again.

Sian can use any elevator—they all go to eight. It's only this one that goes to the remaining floors in the building. Sian touches the red three on the wall once more, plants his palm flat against the smooth curve of the back of the number, the way his hand curled against Theo's back, the way he'd once pressed Theo up against this very wall, nuzzling against his neck and Theo had said, *Don't you think it's about time you marry me?*

Sian presses the button, and waits for the elevator, staring down the smooth white painted hallway leading back to the parking garage. In the elevator, his fingers hover over the eight, over the twelve, his fingertips graze the lines on the two and oh god, how he wants to press the button and take the long, slow ride to the twelfth floor where Theo would be waiting, perhaps eating takeout or a frozen dinner as he used to before Sian started cooking for him.

Perhaps the trip would rewind Sian's mistakes. At floor two, the screaming fight would disappear. At six, Sian's sneering comments about Theo's neediness will disappear. And somewhere between when Sian didn't get off on eight and before the doors opened on twelve, Sian could hit erase on the moment he said, with no uncertainty, *Theo, I will never, ever marry you.*

"Bucky's waiting," Sian says aloud, and he's been alone all day. He jabs at the eight, presses it twice to be sure. The elevator lifts and by floor two, Sian's thinking of the time Theo held a watermelon to his ear, tapping it to discern for ripeness before admitting, with a sheepish grin, that he had no idea what he was listening for. And he's passing the fifth floor, and Theo once fell and cracked his head on the bathroom cabinet and Sian barely breathed all night as he hovered and watched for signs of concussion. The elevator doors open on eight and Sian holds his breath, but his feet won't move. The doors close and Sian's fingers go back to the panel and he's pressing the twelve. He's on nine and Theo taught Sian how to fly a kite, how to release it at just the right moment so it catches the wind and by ten, Sian is laughing, remembering the way it felt to run, the string tugging his hands, while Theo cheered, and the doors open on twelve and Sian is running.

Theo opens the door, his eyes red, his face hard and he stares at Sian who's trying to catch his breath through tears, and he knows he doesn't have a right to ask, but he drops to his knees on the rough carpet outside door 1201 and he says, *Theo will you marry me?*

Things Your Mother Never Told You (Because She Didn't Think You Were Stupid Enough to Do Them)

1. Don't get into a car with men who are high on cocaine and ride across state lines to a nightclub playing music so loud no one can hear you when you say, I want to go home, can you please take me home, I really want to go home now.

2. Don't seek solace in the corner of the dark club, afraid to call your best friend, your mom, or your older sister because you shouldn't have gotten in the car in the first place, because you don't want to bother them at this hour of the night, because you're not entirely sure they'll drive two hours to get you.

3. Don't make eye contact with a woman who gives you an awkward smile. Don't let your eyes fall on her Star Trek shirt, her Levi's, her long fingers. Don't tell her the truth when she asks why you're hiding in the corner. Don't accept her offer to take you home.

4. Don't ask her favourite food or tell her yours when she asks you the same. Don't say yes when she asks you to look at a picture of her cats, Mr. Bojangles and Schwartzie. Don't coo over the cats, ask questions, or look at that little mole on her left cheek and long to touch it. Don't wonder what it would be like to kiss a woman, so soft, so different from the men you've dated.

5. Don't give your number when she asks for it at the end of the night, don't close yourself in your

dorm room, smiling, clutching your teddy bear. Don't tell your roommate you just met the nicest person, how they didn't even try to touch you, how they stayed in the car and watched until you swiped your card at the lobby, made it safely to the light by the mailbox, turned around to wave from behind the locked door. Do pretend not to notice when your roommate lifts her eyebrows at your use of ambiguous pronouns.

6. Don't snatch the phone on the first ring, don't laugh at her jokes, don't say yes when she asks you on a date. For God's sake, don't spend five hours at a café, discussing everything under the sun from Margaret Atwood to tiramisu. Don't twine your fingers together, don't share pieces of cake from one plate, don't kiss gently at the end of the day before running back into the lobby, taking the stairs two at a time, flopping into your bed and crying with happiness.

7. Don't think of her day and night, don't go on a second date, don't meet Mr. Bojangles and Schwartzie, don't introduce her to your cat, Francine or bring Francine to her apartment to see if the cats will get along. Don't let her court you, take you on a trip to Chicago, go to your first pride festival, wave a rainbow flag, get your face painted, and sit on her broad shoulders to see over the crowd. And don't take her home to meet your parents who act overly effusive as if to prove their progressiveness, don't go to her parents' cabin in Vermont where her mom calls you darling and her dad asks what you plan to do with your life. For heaven's sake, don't say yes when she asks you to marry her.

8. Don't buy a house, pick out furniture, learn each other's favourite meals, debate who gets the blue toothbrush. Don't buy a car, then another—don't make playlists together for road trips, don't pack snacks, unwrap cheese sticks for her while she's driving, and sing 80s music at the top of your lungs.

9. Don't stroke the side of her wrist when she reaches for your hand in the car. Don't slide your arms around her neck while she's playing World of Warcraft. Don't scream with delight when she pulls you into her lap, when she nuzzles her face into your hair, when she kisses you in that way that makes your toes curl. Don't hang your wedding pictures right above the mantel surrounded by pictures of Schwartzie, Mr. Bojangles, and Francine, now all passed. Don't adopt new cats together, don't pick names over shots of Jack Daniels, don't invite all your friends over to meet the new cats, Mr. Fuzzybum and Scott Harris. Don't cry for hours in the lobby of a fertilization doctor because it won't make the process any faster and don't press yourself against her when the link finally turns blue and you realize all the money, all the years were not in vain.

10. Don't make your homemade marinara sauce just because it's her favourite and she hasn't been eating well lately. Don't curse when you pull on your favourite jeans and the button is getting tight, don't press your hand to your heart when she says you're as beautiful now as you were the day she first saw you. Don't ask if she'll love you forever, and swoon into her arms when she says she's loved you for all of time. Don't curl her hand over the bowl of your belly and look up to see her crying.

11. Don't ask if she's losing weight, don't question why she's so tired. Don't counsel her to see the doctor. Don't wait for the bloodwork together, don't answer the phone, don't ask about options, don't sit by her bedside holding her hand, don't breathe with her, willing each breath to keep coming, don't hold your breath when hers stops until your head swims and you pass out, falling from the chair and banging your head on the side of the bed.

12. Don't stand next to her wailing mother, holding your swollen belly. Don't sit in the bottom of the closet, face buried in her clothes, breathing in her rapidly fading scent. Don't cry her name when you give birth to your daughter, don't fall in love, don't ever fall in love, just don't ever ever ever fall in love.

About the Author

Finnian Burnett lives in British Columbia where they write stories, take walks, and watch an awful lot of Star Trek. Finnian's work has been published in Writer's Digest, Blank Spaces Magazine, Geist, CBC Books, and more.

www.finnburnett.com

The Price of Cookies (2024) is also available from Off Topic Publishing and wherever books and ebooks are sold.

More Books from Off Topic Publishing

All titles available at

offtopicpublishing.com/shop

or from your usual ebook vendors

The Price of Cookies, by Finnian Burnett

Two brothers face their mother's impending death. A convenience store clerk balances compassion with duty. A grieving soldier receives a package of cookies meant for someone else.

In this series of connected flash fiction pieces, people navigate the trials of life with tears, arguments and, above all, love and compassion.

"This bravura collection of linked stories provides a profound lesson in empathy, of pouring yourself into someone else's life, someone else's pain, to see it from the inside, looking out." - Will Ferguson, Giller Prize-winning author of *419*

Baggage Claim, by Marion Lougheed

By the time Marion Lougheed turned eighteen, she'd moved house eleven times. When she was seven, her family flew from Canada to Benin. Later they moved back to Canada, and then to Belgium and Germany. She went to school in three languages. This poetry collection is for all her fellow child migrants, third culture kids, hippie kids, cross-culture kids, missionary kids, foster kids, refugees, military brats, and other displaced, uprooted, and mobile children. Original illustrations by Sarah Balsley, an artist with a mobile childhood of her own.

"These poems . . . speak to the quiet grief of leaving and the ache of never fully arriving. And yet, threaded through every page is a ... belief that we can keep finding ourselves, piece by piece, no matter how far we've travelled." – Chanel Sutherland, Winner of the Commonwealth Short Story Prize, *Layaway Child*

All Forgotten Now, by Jennifer Mariani

In these poems, Jennifer Mariani grieves a life she can't return to, as she struggles to belong elsewhere. This work explores the reality of growing up white in post-independence Zimbabwe: Jennifer's own privilege juxtaposed with everyday poverty and racism. The poems in this book cry out with grief and rage and loss, and sometimes celebration. Every page is warm with the heat of Africa and wet with the tears of unbelonging.

"[A] stirring collection." – Yejide Kilanko, bestselling author of *Daughters Who Walk This Path* and *A Good Name*

Wayward & Upward: Stories & Poems

A woman runs from a cult leader.

A man watches a crowd carry a baby into the woods.

A boy makes a childhood friend who is much older than she appears.

The forty pieces in this book unite two creative endeavours at the heart of humanity: making music and telling stories.

"Metafictional conversations and stand-alone pieces alike shine with creativity, taking thought experiments to a whole other level of engagement." – Michelle Butler Hallett, Winner of the Thomas Raddall Atlantic Fiction Prize, *Constant Nobody*

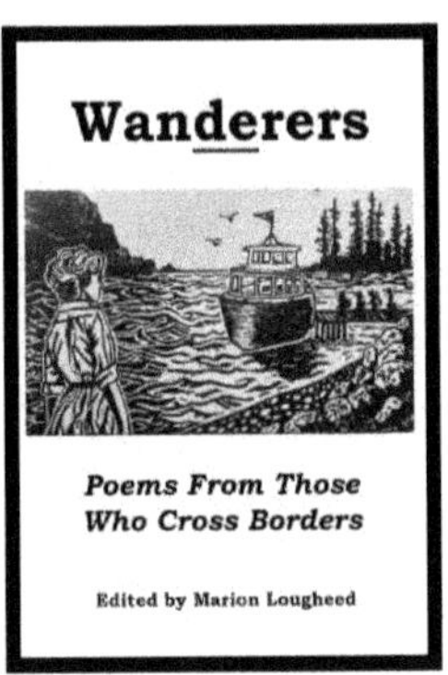

Wanderers:
Poems From Those Who Cross Borders

Whether seeking asylum, travelling between homes, or studying abroad, these poems shimmer and roar with the chaos, beauty and astonishment that come with crossing borders. The impetus for crossing varies, but whatever the reason, borders loom large in the lives of these poets.

"Everyone's experience of borders is different, and beautiful. Read this book." - Mary Grace van der Kroef, author of *The Branch That I Am*

Exhaustion: Limited Reserves

Used up or worn out. Reaching the limits of our personal and collective resources. Laying waste to the planet. Burning fuel until there's nothing left but fumes. Each story and poem in this book engages exhaustion anew, revealing human struggles, moments of grace, and a relentless questioning.

"Society pressures us to carry stress, even when it weighs more than we do. These pieces reflect that common experience and give words to the silent struggles that isolate us within ourselves." - Renee Cronley, nurse and author of *Burnout*

Home: An Anthology

What is home? Is it a place? A feeling? A person? Does it shift and change? Can you point towards it but never quite attain it? Through poems and flash fiction from diverse voices, this anthology wrestles with the complexities of belonging.

“The voice came again. ‘You are welcome here, Jia, if you are as committed to peace as you claim. Come and take refuge.’” - from "Refuge" by Dawn Vogel (short story in *Home*)

Standing Up: A Charity Anthology for Ukraine

You rose up: against tyranny, convention, rudeness, unfavourable odds, malevolence, apathy. Against your boss, your barista, your worst enemy, your best friend, yourself. You saved the day. Actually, maybe made things worse. Made a difference. Got flattened. Did it work? Well, life's complicated. But one thing's for sure: On that day, you saw something you believed was wrong and you took action.

This anthology's proceeds will be 100% donated to the Canada-Ukraine Foundation.

www.ingramcontent.com/pod-product-compliance
Ingram Content Group UK Ltd.
Pitfield, Milton Keynes, MK11 3LW, UK
UKHW020416250726
13967UKWH00007B/2678

9 781069 834409